BRIGHT
IDEA
BOOKS

MARINE
Biologist

by Marne Ventura

CAPSTONE PRESS
a capstone imprint

Bright Idea Books are published by Capstone Press
1710 Roe Crest Drive, North Mankato, Minnesota 56003
www.mycapstone.com

Library of Congress Cataloging-in-Publication Data
Names: Ventura, Marne, author.
Title: Marine biologist / by Marne Ventura.
Description: North Mankato, Minnesota : Capstone Press, 2019. | Series: Jobs
  with animals | Includes bibliographical references and index. | Audience:
  Age 9-12. | Audience: Grade 4 to 6.
Identifiers: LCCN 2018035987 | ISBN 9781543557848 (hardcover : alk. paper) |
  ISBN 9781543558166 (ebook) | ISBN 9781543560466 (paperback)
Subjects: LCSH: Marine biologists--Juvenile literature. | Marine
  biology--Juvenile literature. | Vocational guidance--Juvenile literature.
Classification: LCC QH91.45 .V46 2019 | DDC 578.77--dc23
LC record available at https://lccn.loc.gov/2018035987

Editorial Credits
Editor: Meg Gaertner
Designer: Becky Daum
Production Specialist: Dan Peluso

Photo Credits
iStockphoto: damircudic, 18–19, gracethang, 31, jsteck, 24–25, 28, kali9, 17, Rainer von Brandis, 9, Wavebreakmedia, 21; Shutterstock Images: Abd. Halim Hadi, 14, Dan Logan, 11, frantisekhojdysz, 23, James Kirkikis, 26, kunanon, 13, Levent Konuk, 20, lmfoto, 14–15, Nicole Helgason, 7, Rich Carey, cover, Rizd, 5, Tabby Mittins, 26–27, zaferkizilkaya, 10

Printed in the United States of America.
PA48

TABLE OF CONTENTS

CHAPTER 1

MARINE Biologist

Dolphins swim in the ocean. A boat follows them. A woman watches from the boat. She sees where the dolphins go.

The woman writes down notes.
She collects water samples. She tests
the water. She is a **marine biologist**.
She studies life in the sea.

Marine biologists
get to spend time
with marine wildlife.

OCEAN LIFE

There are many forms of sea life. Biologists choose which to study. Some study sea animals. They study tiny fish. They study huge whales. They watch how the animals behave. Others study ocean plants. They study long kelp. They study seagrass. They study how animals and plants live together. The biologists collect **data**. They study it. They write papers about what they find.

THE OCEAN

About 70 percent of Earth is covered by water. More than 96 percent of the water is in the ocean.

Marine biologists studying coral might measure its size.

Lab work might include looking at seawater samples.

INDOOR WORK

Marine biologists work indoors too. They work in labs. They enter data into computers. They do studies to learn about sea life. They write papers. They give talks. They share their **research** with others.

Scientists may give talks to classes, other scientists, and the public.

CHAPTER 3

EDUCATION

Marine biologists go to college. They study for four years. They get a **degree**. Then most go to graduate school. This might take another four or more years.

Some colleges offer a degree in marine **biology**. These colleges are near the ocean. Students can also study biology. They can study **zoology**.

Students might study the bones of marine animals. This skeleton is from a bottlenose dolphin.

- Class Mammalia

LEARNING SKILLS

Marine biologists gain skills in school. They take science classes. They take math classes. They learn good computer skills. These skills help them study data. They practice writing and speaking skills too. They write research papers. They explain their findings to others.

Marine biology students might take diving lessons so they can explore underwater.

In some science classes, students go outside and collect data.

PLENTY TO LEARN

About 95 percent of the sea is unexplored. There are many regions, plants, and animals to study.

CHAPTER 4

GETTING Experience

School is not the only way to get experience. You can prepare for the work now. Learn all you can about sea life. It might help you get a job later.

Some cities have
marine parks that
people can visit.

OTHER WAYS TO LEARN

Many cities have an **aquarium**. Visit it often. Learn about the animals. Ask questions. Some aquariums have programs for students. People can take classes. Some aquariums also take **volunteers**. They may hire students to work for them.

Visitors can see marine animals and plants at the aquarium.

There are movies and TV shows about different marine plants and animals.

There are many things you can do from home. Watch TV shows about ocean life. Read books about the sea. Search online for more facts. These activities will help prepare you for your future work.

Local libraries will have books about marine life.

21

CHAPTER 5

WHERE THEY Work

There are many jobs for marine biologists. Finding a job might mean moving to a new place. Not all ocean scientists live near the ocean. But they spend time there for their work.

Marine biologists often travel to be near the plants and animals they study.

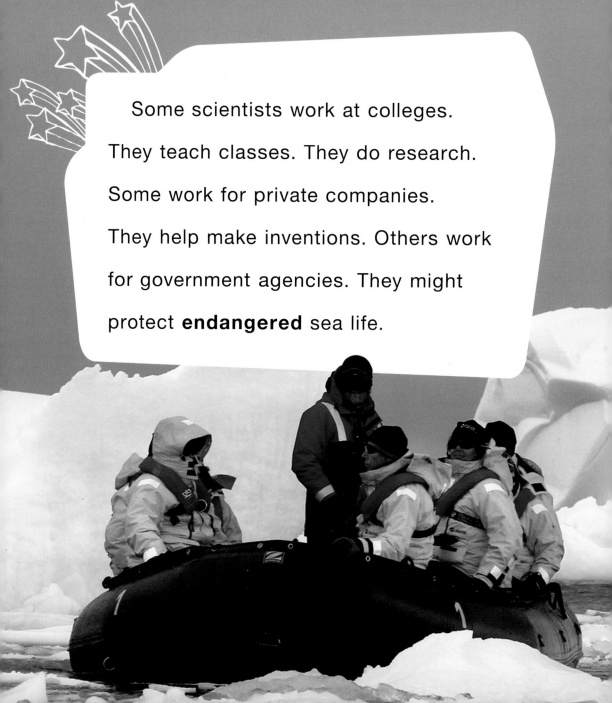

Some scientists work at colleges. They teach classes. They do research. Some work for private companies. They help make inventions. Others work for government agencies. They might protect **endangered** sea life.

Marine biologists might focus on a particular region of the world, such as Antarctica.

SHARK SKIN

One company studied the skin of sharks. The skin has tiny bumps. Germs cannot spread easily on it. Scientists used what they learned. They made doorknobs that germs will not stick to.

Aquariums also hire marine biologists. Zoos do too. The scientists keep the sea life safe. They teach visitors about the plants and animals.

Marine biologists help take care of aquarium animals.

Some marine biologists study endangered animals, such as sea turtles.

Marine biologists make $50,000 per year on average. Their pay depends on where they work. But they all get to work with sea life.

GLOSSARY

aquarium
a place where water plants and animals are kept for people to look at

biologist
a scientist who studies living things

biology
the study of life

data
facts or information

degree
an academic title given to students after they complete a course of study

endangered
in danger of dying out

marine
related to the sea

research
study or investigation

volunteer
someone who works without pay

zoology
the study of the behavior and physical traits of animals

OTHER JOBS TO CONSIDER

MARINE ANIMAL TRAINER

Animal trainers work at parks and zoos. They train animals to perform in shows. They might work with dolphins or sea lions. They teach the animals tricks.

MARINE BIOTECHNOLOGIST

Marine biotechnologists study sea life. They use what they learn to make inventions. They work for private companies.

ZOOKEEPER

Zookeepers take care of animals in zoos. They often focus on one type of animal. They feed and exercise the animals. They teach zoo visitors about the animals.

ACTIVITY

MARINE BIOLOGIST FOR A DAY

Pretend you are a marine biologist. Choose an ocean animal to study. What do you want to know about that animal? Decide on a single specific question. Go to your local library. Read books about that animal. Use online resources to learn more. Keep searching until you find the answer to your question.

Write a report about what you learned. First, mention the specific question that you had. Next, describe how you got the answer. Then describe the answer itself. Write about any conclusions you had. Share your paper with family and friends. Give a brief talk on what you learned.

FURTHER RESOURCES

Want to be a marine biologist? Learn more here:

PBS Learning Media: Marine Biologist
https://tpt.pbslearningmedia.org/resource/9457fa09-b5af-46d3-b7fb-
    d241670ef463/9457fa09-b5af-46d3-b7fb-d241670ef463/

Science Buddies: Marine Biologist
www.sciencebuddies.org/science-engineering-careers/life-sciences/marine-
    biologist

Curious about related jobs? Check out these resources:

Bedell, J. M. *So, You Want to Work with Animals? Discover Fantastic Ways to
    Work with Animals, from Veterinary Science to Aquatic Biology.* New York:
    Aladdin, 2017.

Monterey Bay Aquarium: Career Resources
www.montereybayaquarium.org/education/teen-career-resources

Science News for Students: Eureka! Lab
www.sciencenewsforstudents.org/blog/eureka-lab/these-scientists-study-
    plants-and-animals-land-and-sea

INDEX